WELCOME TO THE ANCIENT FAR NORTH... AND THE WORLD OF THE MICEKINGS!

WHERE THEY LIVE: Miceking Island

CAPITAL: Mouseborg, home of the Stiltonord family

OTHER VILLAGES: Oofadale, village of the Oofa Oofa, and Feargard, village of the vilekings

CLIMATE: Cold, cold, cold, especially when the icy north wind blows!

TYPICAL FOOD: Gloog, a superstinky but fabumouse stew. The secret recipe is closely guarded by the wife of the miceking chief.

NATIONAL DRINK: Finnbrew, made of equal parts codfish juice and herring juice, with a splash of squid ink

MEANS OF TRANSPORTATION: The drekar, a light but very fast ship

GREATEST HONOR: The miceking helmet. It is only earned when a mouse performs an act of courage or wins a Miceking Challenge.

UNIT OF MEASUREMENT: A mouseking tail (full tail, half tail, third tail, quarter tail)

ENEMIES: The terrible dragons who live in Beastgard

MEET THE STILTONORD FAMILY ...

GERONIMO
Advisor to the
miceking chief.

THEA
A horse trainer who
works well with all kinds
of animals

TRAP
The most famouse
inventor in Mouseborg

BENJAMIN
Geronimo's nephew

BUGSILDA
Benjamin's best
friend

... AND THE EVIL DRAGONS!

The dragons are divided into 5 clans, all of which are terrifying!

1. Devourers
They love to eat micekings raw — no cooking necessary.

2. Steamers
They grab micekings, then fly over volcanoes so the steam and smoke make them taste good.

3. Biters
Before eating micekings, they nibble them delicately to see if they like them or not.

4. Slurpers
They wrap their long tongues around micekings and slurp them up.

5. Rinsers
As soon as they catch micekings, they rinse them in a stream to wash them off.

Geronimo Stilton

MICEKINGS

THE HELMET HOLDUP

Scholastic Inc.

Published by Scholastic Inc., *Publishers since 1920*, 557 Broadway, New York, NY 10012. SCHOLASTIC and associated logos are trademarks and/or registered trademarks of Scholastic Inc.

Stilton is the name of a famous English cheese. It is a registered trademark of the Stilton Cheese Makers' Association. For more information, go to www.stiltoncheese.com.

This book is a work of fiction. Names, characters, places, and incidents are either the product of the author's imagination or are used fictitiously, and any resemblance to actual persons, living or dead, business establishments, events, or locales is entirely coincidental.

ISBN 978-1-338-15921-9

Text by Geronimo Stilton
Original title *Chi ha rubato l'elmo topingo?*
Cover by Giuseppe Facciotto (pencils) and Flavio Ferron (ink and color)
Illustrations by Giuseppe Facciotto (pencils) and Alessandro Costa (ink and color)
Graphics by Chiara Cebraro

Special thanks to AnnMarie Anderson
Translated by Andrea Schaffer
Interior design by Becky James

10 9 8 7 6 5 4 3 2 1   17 18 19 20 21

Printed in the U.S.A.   40
First printing 2017

I'M MOUSETASTICALLY LATE!

It was a beautiful summer **afternoon** in Mouseborg, the capital of Miceking Island. The **sky** was clear, there was a light breeze blowing, and seagulls fluttered around the dock, squawking **happily**.

Oh, I'm so sorry! I haven't introduced myself: My name is Geronimo Stiltonord, and I am a mouseking scholar.

On this day, every mouseking in Mouseborg was looking forward to that evening's special performance by the THREE MOUSEKINGETEERS. Who are they,

THE THREE MOUSEKINGETEERS

Chucklepaw

Snickerfur

Gigglewhiskers

Their names are Chucklepaw, Snickerfur, and Gigglewhiskers. They have curly red hair and wear super-stylish clothes, just like true celebrities!

you ask? Only the most famouse comics on Miceking Island!

The show was planned for sunset in Great Stone Square. **SVEN tHE SHOUtEr**, our village chief, had decided that I, *GERONIMO STILTONORD*, would be the announcer for the performance! So, that evening, I put on my fanciest cloak, combed my fur and whiskers, and splashed on some **Eau de Mousk** cologne.

I opened the door to my house and glanced up at the sky before I stepped outside. I was checking to make sure there were no **dragons** in sight. Luckily, everything was calm — at least in the sky! But as I walked toward the center of the village, mice all around me were nervously *DASHING* here and there.

I figured they were hurrying toward Great

Stone Square because they were worried about getting good seats for the show!

Wait a minute . . . the show was about to begin. That's why everyone was in such a rush. But the show couldn't possibly start without me!

"Helmets and herring, I'm mousetastically late!" I squeaked.

I'm late!

I scampered through the village at record-breaking **speed**. I had just passed Sven the Shouter's house when someone suddenly appeared in front of me, blocking my path.

BONKKK!!

We ran right into each other!

Let's go!

Hurry!

ARE YOU FOLLOWING US?

A second later I was surrounded by three mice as big as **GRAY SEALS**. They crowded around me menacingly and got right up in my snout.

"Whoa," I said, trying to remain friendly. "Give a mouse a little room to squeak, please!"

"Are you **following** us?" one of the mice growled at me.

"N-no, of c-course not!" I stuttered.

I looked closely at the three mice. They

GRAY SEAL

were very large and they had enormouse muscles. The hair on their heads was **curly** and **bright red**, and they wore long cloaks decorated with **seashells**.

"Who are you?" I asked, my whiskers trembling nervously.

Great groaning glaciers! It was the Three Mousckingeteers — **Chucklepaw**, **Snickerfur**, and **Gigglewhiskers**!

Are you following us?

Well?

Answer us!

Immediately, I felt **calmer**.

"Who are we?" the first mouse replied. "Who are **YOU**?"

"My name is *GERONIMO STILTONORD*," I explained. "I am an advisor to the great Sven the Shouter."

The three mice took a step back.

"Okay, smarty-mouseking," the second mouse squeaked. "But what do you want from **US**?"

"Nothing!" I replied, perplexed. "I'm just trying to get to GREAT STONE SQUARE. You see, I'm announcing your show tonight!"

The three mice glanced at one another and a confused look passed between them.

"But of course, the show!" the first one said suddenly.

"Uh, yes, of course," the second one added. "In fact, we were about to go get, uh . . ."

". . . to get our costumes, **OBVIOUSLY**!" the third mouse finished.

"Now, please get out of our way," the first mouse said. "We really must get out of here!"

"Ahem, yes," the second mouse added quickly. "And by 'get out of here,' we mean, we have to hurry! Don't want to be late for our own show."

The three mice **chuckled** nervously.

How strange! The Three Mousekingeteers seemed as anxious as first-time performers!

I was late, too, so I quickly said good-bye.

"See you onstage!" I squeaked as I scurried off.

Just a few steps later . . . **WHOOPS**! I tripped over a shiny miceking helmet. Maybe you don't know it, but miceking helmets are given to those who distinguish themselves with strength and character. It's the GREATEST HONOR, and one I had yet to receive!

I picked up the helmet.

Huh?!

Is this yours?

"Wait!" I called after the Mousekingeteers. "Is this yours?"

The three mice exchanged a glance. Then Chucklepaw immediately grabbed the helmet from me.

"Oh yes," he replied quickly. "**Thanks!** See you later, smarty-mouseking!"

Then they scurried away, **snickering**.

What strange mice!

A moment later, a loud shout nearly made me jump out of my fur.

"GERONIMOOOOO! WHERE ARE YOU? THE SHOW IS ABOUT TO BEGIN!"

It was Sven the Shouter! In case you haven't figured it out, he yells very, very **loudly**!

Squeak! I had to **move it**!

Presenting the Three Mousekingeteers!

I arrived at Great Stone Square just as Sven stepped onto the stage.

"Citizens of Mouseborg," he roared. "The great comedy show is about to begin."

"**Hooray!**" the crowd shouted.

"You'll split your sides laughing!" Sven cried. "**SO SAYS SVEN THE SHOUTER!**"

As is customary in Mouseborg, the crowd echoed back:

"SO SAYS SVEN THE SHOUTER!"

Then Sven noticed me in the crowd.

"You're finally here, Geronimo!" he

boomed. "Come on! You need to introduce the THREE MOUSEKINGETEERS!"

I joined him on the stage.

"Welcome to this evening of entertainment, art, and laughter," I began. "It is a great honor to present . . ."

I paused as the mice in the square grumbled:

It is a great honor . . .

"Will this take long?"

"We're as bored as herring in brine!"

"We want the comics!"

But my sister Thea made a sign from the wing of the stage for me to continue squeaking. If I had understood her gestures correctly, the Mousekingeteers hadn't arrived yet!

But Sven was also motioning to me from

the wing. He wanted me to S+☉P squeaking, because everyone was impatient to see the show!

HELMETS AND HERRING!

I didn't know what to do!

"Well . . . anyway . . ." I muttered, trying my best to continue. "The show you are about to see features the most famous **comics** in Mouseborg . . . uh, I mean on Miceking Island . . ."

But the crowd continued to complain:

"ENOUGH, SMARTY-MOUSEKING!"

"WE WANT THE THREE MOUSEKINGETEERS!"

"This is so boring, I'm falling asleep standing up!"

We want the comics!
Enough!
Cut it short!
No, take your time!
How boring!

Offstage, I saw Thea whisper something into Sven's ear. His eyes grew wide with shock. Now he, too, knew that the comics hadn't arrived yet!

"**CRUSTY CODFISH, DO SOMETHING, GERONIMO!**" Sven shouted. "**ENTERTAIN THE PUBLIC!**"

I couldn't believe my ears.

"M-me?" I squeaked.

"Yes, you!" Sven yelled loudly. "Tell some **JOKES**, that's an **order**! So says Sven the Shouter!"

"SO SAYS SVEN THE SHOUTER!"

the crowd replied.

Shivering squids, I don't know how to tell jokes!

Then Sven gave me a look that was **SHARPER** than a **SWORD**. So I did my best . . .

16

"One sea mouse said to another:
'Yesterday I went fishing in the
frozen fjord.'
'Oh yeah?' the mouse replied. 'And what
did you catch?'
'A nice cold!'"

The mice in the crowd stared at me, their eyes wide. But **no one** laughed! I tried another one:

"Why wouldn't the shrimp share his toys
with his friend?
Because he was a little shellfish!"

The crowd began to shout:

"**Boooooooooo!**"

Fjords and fiddlesticks! I never said I was good at telling JOKES!

"Psst, Geronimo — catch!" Thea squeaked

as she tossed me four **PINECONES**. "Juggle them!"

I tried my best, but I was **terrible**. First I dropped one on my LEFT paw. Then I dropped one on my RIGHT. A third pinecone bonked me on the snout. **OUCH!**

The public had had enough. I had to get off that stage before they pelted me with rotten fish!

Then Sven's wife, Mousehilde, **saved** me.

"Sven!" she yelled. "I need to squeak with you. **IT'S AN EMERGENCY!**"

WHO STOLE THE HELMET?

Sven quickly made his way through the crowd toward his wife.

"What happened?" he asked her worriedly.

"Oh, Sven!" she squeaked. "MICEKING HELMET NUMBER FORTY-EIGHT has disappeared from your private collection!"

"WHAAAAAT?!"

Mousehilde nodded. "When I got home, the door was open and —"

Sven's snout turned purple with rage.

"So someone broke into our house to STEAL it?!" he cried.

"**OOOOOOOOOOHHH!**" exclaimed the crowd.

"This is **terrible**," Sven shouted angrily. "That's one's of my **favorites**! I, Sven the Shouter, order every citizen of Mouseborg to search for my missing helmet — now! **SO SAYS SVEN THE SHOUTER!**"

"**SO SAYS SVEN THE SHOUTER!**" the crowd echoed.

While the crowd dispersed to search every corner of the city, I approached the chief timidly.

"Er, excuse me, Mr. Sven . . ." I squeaked.

"Not now, Mr. Smarty-Mouseking!" he replied, brushing me off. "**I'M BUSY!**"

"Sorry, Chief," I persisted. "It's just that no one knows what helmet number forty-eight LOOKS LIKE!"

"Well, why didn't you say something before?!" Sven bellowed. Then he pawed me a **banner** with the image of the helmet on it. Hmmm . . . it looked so **FAMILIAR**. Where had I seen that helmet before?

Crusty codfish! It looked just like the one I had returned to the THREE MOUSEKINGETEERS!

Uh-oh. Sven wasn't going to be happy when I told him! I tried to back up slowly. If I could just slip into the crowd . . .

"Where do you think you're going, smarty-mouseking?" Sven demanded. He stood directly in front

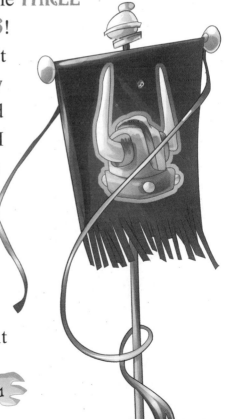

of me, **blocking** my path. "Do you know something about my helmet?"

"W-well, I think, uh, maybe, er, I saw it, um . . ."

"Come on!" Sven shouted **impatiently**. "Spit it out, mouseking!"

"I saw the Three Mousekingeteers drop it

right in front of your house," I explained. "Come to think of it, those three were acting very, very **STRANGELY** . . ."

"Great groaning glaciers!" Sven yelled. "**THERE'S NOT A MOMENT TO LOSE!** We must go after them. The Three Mousekingeteers are the **thieves**!"

THE HUNT FOR THE COMICS

We sped through the streets of Mouseborg searching for the three comedians. Along the way, we found an odd trail of *clothing* along the ground that included three **RED WIGS** and three **CLOAKS** covered in seashells. It looked like the Three Mousekingeteers had changed clothes very quickly.

The trail of costumes led us right to the inn where the Three Mousekingeteers were staying. **How strange!**

Sven knocked, but there was no answer. Then he pushed open the door.

"Show your snouts, thieves!" he yelled. "Why did you steal my favorite **HELMET**?"

But Mousehilde just gasped. The Three Mouskingeteers were tied up and gagged! "Sven, they can't be the thieves," she said. "Look at them!"

"And these aren't the **three mice** I met earlier with the helmet," I added.

Sven untied them right away.

"Tell us what happened," he demanded.

The first mouse began. "Well, right after we arrived in Mouseborg this morning, someone knocked on our door," he explained. "When we opened it, we were greeted by **THREE VILEKINGS**!"

My whiskers shivered with fright. No mouse wants to have anything to do with the evil vilekings . . . they're like **PIRATES**, only way worse!

"They tied us up and stole our costumes," the second mouse said.

THE VILEKINGS

The Vilekings are disrespectful mice who fight with everyone. They ATTACK ships as they enter the harbor and try to STEAL their cargo.

Their village, FEARFJORD, is a very scary place. It faces a gulf full of sharp reefs and very ferocious sharks. Their village chief is RATNOLF THE TERRIBLE. He rules with an iron paw!

RATNOLF THE TERRIBLE

"They took our **RED** wigs and our 𝔟𝔢𝔞𝔲𝔱𝔦𝔣𝔲𝔩 cloaks!" the third Mousekingeteer squeaked.

The vilekings had used the ſtolen costumes to disguise themselves as the Three Mouskingeteers. Then they had stolen Sven's favorite helmet. I must have met them right as they were getting away!

VILEKING   CLOAK   FAKE
WIG   MOUSEKINGETEER

HELMETS AND HERRING!

It had happened right under my whiskers!

But there was one thing I didn't **understand**.

"Why did they only steal **one HeLMeT** from the collection?" I asked timidly.

"I know why!" Sven exclaimed "I earned miceking helmet number forty-eight during the famous **Battle of the Twenty-One Dragons**. But Ratnolf the Terrible claimed he was the winner of the battle — and the helmet!"

"It's true," Mousehilde agreed. "The vileking chief has always insisted that he defeated the **last dragon**. But I was there, and I **know** it was Sven!"

"Exactly!" Sven thundered. "This isn't

just a theft — it's a **CHALLENGE!**"

Right at that moment, we were joined by Sven's daughter, Thora.

Oh, Thora! She is the most fascinating, athletic, and courageous **mouse** in Mouseborg, and I might have a <u>teeny, tiny crush</u> on her!

"Don't worry, Dad," Thora told her father. "I will **VOLUNTEER** for this mouseking mission. I will find your mouseking helmet, and I will return it to its rightful home — Mouseborg!"

"Well said, my **courageous** daughter!" Sven said approvingly. "I will prepare all your equipment for the expedition **myself**!"

Then he turned and clapped a gigantic paw on my shoulder.

"And you will accompany her!" he shouted.

I began to shake from the tips of my whiskers to the end of my tail.

"But, but, but . . . w-why m-me?" I stammered.

"Did you forget that this is **ALL YOUR FAULT**?" Sven's voice **BOOMED**. "You didn't recognize the vilekings! And you didn't stop them from stealing my MOUSEKING HELMET! The theft happened right under your whiskers! You're going with Thora, and that's an order. So says Sven the Shouter!"

"OOHHH!" the small crowd around us cried.

"SO SAYS SVEN THE SHOUTER!"

"Now, hurry to the port!" Sven ordered.

"Olaf the Fearless will take you on his drekar, the Bated Breath!"

Crusty codfish, why me?

Every time I go on a mouseking mission, I have to travel on Olaf's stinky <u>longship</u>. At least this time I was going with the **magnificent** Thora!

ANCHORS AWEIGH!

When I arrived at the port, the sun had already disappeared into the **sea**.

"Excuse me," I asked a sailor with his back to me, "but have you seen Olaf the Fearless or his **stinky** longship, uh . . . I mean, the *Bated Breath*?"

The sailor giggled in reply. "Good evening, Cousin!" he squeaked. "I was actually **waiting** for you!"

In the dark, I hadn't recognized my cousin Trap.

He's the **village inventor**, and he can be a real pain in my tail. Who knows what he wanted from me!

"Trap, if you want me to **test** an

invention, forget it!" I squeaked.

"I'm here to **help** you, Geronimo," he replied. "I'm going, too! Isn't that *great*?!"

Shivering squids!

My cousin is usually more of a troublemaker than a helper. Before I could ask why he wanted to come, Olaf the Fearless appeared beside me.

We're off!

He pinched my ear and steered me onto his ship.

"Anchors aweigh!" he shouted. "We're leaving!"

"Captain, uh, I'm not sure this is such a GOOD idea," I squeaked as he dragged me along. "You see, I suffer from terrible SEASICKNESS!"

Olaf just smoothed out his whiskers.

"Oh, no problem!" he said. "Even if you're seasick, you can still

1 mop the deck or

2 MEND the sails or

3 row, row, row!"

My head was spinning from thinking about all that work.

"Actually, no!" Olaf said suddenly. "I have

another job for you. Climb the **MAIN MAST** and keep an eye on the sea: It's full of dangerously **SHARP** reefs!"

"Can't Trap do it?" I squeaked. "**I'm also afraid of heights!**"

"Blasted barnacles, Geronimo!" Olaf boomed. "Did you think you were going on **vacation**? You will be the lookout! Now climb."

Pant, pant!

3

"You can do it, Geronimo!" Thora said encouragingly.

What choice did I have? Reluctantly, I began to climb the main mast. It was very tall! Have I mentioned that I am **VERY** afraid of heights?!

Meanwhile, the *Bated Breath* let out its sails and headed for FEARFJORD. Everyone was excited about the mission except me. After just a few minutes on board, I smelled worse than the **smelliest** codfish in the sea and the **stinkiest** cheese in Mouseborg — combined!

A few hours later, I suddenly saw something in the water in front of us.

"Land!" I squeaked. "I see laaaaaand!"

"It's Shipwreck Rock!" Olaf replied. "We have arrived at Fearfjord!"

With those words, my paws began to

tremble. Fearfjord is super **FRIGHTENING** and **dangerous**. The water is **dark**, the currents are incredibly **STRONG**, and the fjord is full of rocks as **SHARP** as dragon teeth!

"Pay attention, mollusk!" Olaf called to me as we passed the **WRECKAGE** of a ship. "You don't want to meet the same **fate**, do you?!"

Suddenly, I saw something move on the wreck in front of us. It was a rodent in **trouble**!

"MOUSE OVERBOOOOOARD!"

I squeaked, pointing at the castaway.

STRANDED ON
SHIPWRECK ROCK

The shipwrecked mouse waved frantically, trying to stay afloat and keep his snout above WATER.

Thora threw out a rope and yelled, "We must get closer!"

Meanwhile, I directed Captain Olaf:

"To the RIGHT, to the RIGHT, to the LEFT, to the LEFT . . . no, no, no . . . that's too much . . . watch out!"

CRAAAAAAAAAAASH!

Our ship went ashore on Shipwreck Rock,

right next to the other **WRECK**!

"Blasted barnacles!" Olaf boomed. "This is entirely your fault, Geronimo!" **WHY**, **WHY**, **WHY** does everyone always blame **Me**?

At that point, we were so close to the reef that Thora let out the rope and jumped directly down onto the **sharp surface**. What a courageous mouse!

One after another, we all climbed down. Captain Olaf immediately began to survey the **damage** to his ship.

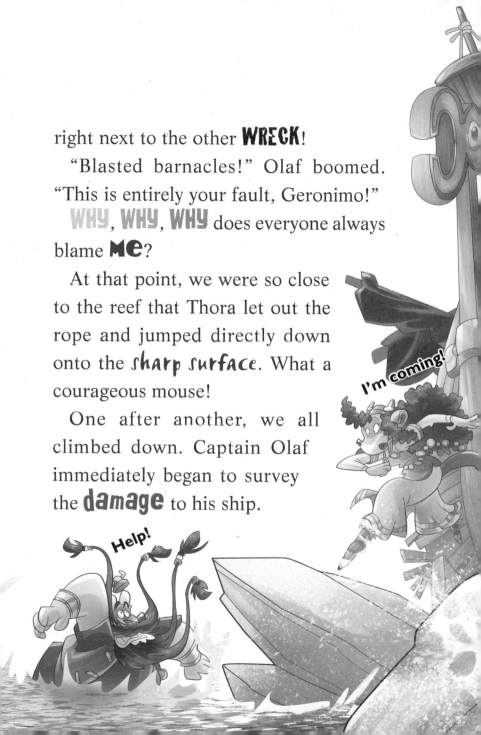

I'm coming!

Help!

TWISTED WHISKER

The Invincible Vileking

Twisted Whisker is one of the most awful vilekings in Fearfjord. He's called invincible because it is said that nothing can stop him. He shatters, smashes, and snatches anything that crosses his path. In other words, it's best not to make him mad!

Get out of my way!

Meanwhile, **Thora** helped the mouse scramble to safety on Shipwreck Rock.

As soon as the mouse saw me, he gasped.

"I know you, **COD SNOUT**!" he cried. "You're that smarty-**MOUSEKING** from Mouseborg!"

I **immediately** recognized him, too.

"That's one of the vileking **thieves**!" I squeaked.

"You and your friends tied up the Three Mouskingeteers

and stole Sven's **HeLMeT**!"

"So you're the one who took my father's helmet!" Thora roared. "Well, we came to take it back!"

"You came this far for nothing, then!" he replied. He stomped his paw on the ground. "You'll find out soon that we vilekings don't like those who **TRESPASS** here!"

"Oh, really?" Thora asked. "If we hadn't helped you, you'd still be **FLOUNDERING** in that cold water! Speaking of which, what happened to you, anyway?"

Twisted Whisker was silent for a moment. Then he decided to tell his **story**:

"I was returning to Fearfjord with my friends after the successful completion of the mission to get the mouseking helmet back —"

"What mission?!" Thora squeaked, interrupting him. "It was a **THEFT**!"

Twisted Whisker ignored her. "As I was saying, we were coming home when we began to **1** argue about who would get the credit for the feat. As we were fighting, **2** the ship got caught on the **reef**.

1

2

"The rest of the crew 3 left aboard the only **lifeboat** on the ship, leaving me behind."

I couldn't believe my ears.

"How could they do that?" I squeaked. "I could never leave a mouse **in danger**!"

"Squeaking of danger . . ." Thora said, her eyes **WIDE** as she looked at the sky behind me.

I turned around and almost fainted with fear!

"**D-D-DraG . . . D-DraaaaGONS!**" I stammered.

WARNING: DRAGONS!

A group of **dragons** passed overhead, flying low over Shipwreck Rock. They were spitting **FIRE** from their mouths and **smoke** from their nostrils.

CHEESY CATAPULTS! They were enormouse, and they looked **hungry**!

Before we could move a whisker, a red dragon **glided** toward us and landed on the deck of the *Bated Breath*. A second later, a green dragon landed next to him. Luckily, they didn't seem to **realize** we were there!

"What are you doing, Crimson?" the green dragon hissed. "Doe**SSS** thi**SSS** seem like the time to re**SSS**t?"

The red dragon stretched his wings. "You'd be tired, too, Chartreuse, if you were as fat and heavy as me!"

We stayed hidden behind the longship, just a few tails away from those FEROCIOUS DRAGONS, hoping they wouldn't see us. The dragons seemed to think the *Bated Breath* was just another one of the many abandoned SHIPWRECKS on the reefs in

I'm tired!

the waters around Fearfjord!

"Well, I'm not tired," Chartreuse replied. "But these long flights do make me **ravenous**!"

"Ye**SSS**, I'm **SSS**tarving, too. I could devour one hundred vileking**SSS** in one **BITE**!" Crimson agreed.

Suddenly, Chartreuse began to sniff the air.

I'm hungry!

Sssniff . . . Sssniff . . .

"Well, we're almo**SSS**t there," he said. "Do you **SSS**mell **SSS**omething?"

"Ye**SSS**," Crimson replied. "I **SSS**mell it, too! I can't wait to bite into a nice, yummy vileking!"

We're almost there!

My tail trembled with fear.

"Squeak!" I exclaimed before I could stop myself.

Hey, lazybonesss!

Crimson swung around.

"Did you hear that?" he roared. "What wa**SSS** it?"

Fortunately, right at that moment, another dragon called to them from above.

"Hey, you two lazybone**SSS**!" the blue dragon bellowed. "Hurry up, or the other**SSS** will gobble up the fattest mice before we arrive!"

Chartreuse seemed irritated.

"That'**SSS** not true, Blue Villain!" he

growled. "Dragon law **SSS**ays that the fattest mice are divided into equal part**SSS** . . ."

Blue Villain snorted a cloud of gray smoke.

"All I know is that if the Devourer**SSS** arrive fir**SSS**t, they won't wait for u**SSS** before they eat the be**SSS**t vileking**SSS**!"'

With that, the dragons took to the skies. They were heading right for the vileking village!

As soon as they were gone, I let out a huge sigh of relief. But Twisted Whisker was **ANGRIER** than ever.

"Those **stinking dragons** are about to attack Fearfjord!" he yelled. "We've got to stop them!"

"Yes, but h-how will we g-get to the village?" I stammered nervously. "Our ship is marooned on Shipwreck Rock . . ."

"Don't be a **shrimp without a shell**,

Geronimo!" Trap shouted. "We can construct a RAFT using some rope and the wooden boards from this wreck!"

"Excellent plan!" Olaf agreed decisively. "We'll set out in the flick of a whisker!"

"But HOW?" I moaned anxiously. Why, oh why, do I always find myself in these **dangerous** situations?

Olaf gave me a pat on the back.

"Here's how: YOU and your friends will set out for Fearfjord while I fix the damage you did to my longship!" he squeaked. "A captain never abandons his SHIP!"

Right at that moment, we heard a dreadful sound from the Cliffs of Fear that overlook the village of Fearfjord:

AAAAAAAH! AAAAAAAH!
AAAAAAAH! AAAAAAAH!

It was the vileking anti-dragon alarm!

I Don't Want to Be Shark Food!

"We have to get out of here!" Twisted Whisker exclaimed. "The dragon **attack** has begun!"

Thora was busy furiously building the raft.

"We'll be ready to *leave* in a minute!" she squeaked.

"Do you think we can trust the vilekings?" Trap **whispered** to me. "After all, they stole Sven's mouseking helmet number forty-eight. It seems **strange** to be helping them . . ."

Thora overheard us. She gave us a look that was **colder** than an iceberg. "Mice must always unite to fight the dragons **together!**" she said sharply.

"It would be easier if they weren't so **irritating** . . ." Trap mumbled in reply.

By now, we had finished assembling the raft, and we headed out for the shore.

The current was very strong, though, and our raft began to bounce **UP** and **DOWN** and **UP** and **DOWN** and **UP** and **DOWN** on the waves . . .

Puff! Pant!

It was so rough, we almost flipped over!
HOW HORRIFYING!

"Geronimo!" Trap yelled. "What are you doing sitting there with your paws up? Help Thora **ROW**!"

"S-so sorry, Thora!" I stammered, jumping up. "Of course I'll help!"

But as I took the oar from Thora, Twisted Whisker jumped in front of me.

he yelled. "I'll be the one to row, because I'm the **STRONGEST**!"

Resigned, I turned to hand him the oar when . . .

BAAAM!

I hit Twisted Whisker directly on the snout!

"Oh!" I exclaimed. "E-excuse me . . . I

didn't mean . . ."

"Be quiet!" he roared. "OR I WILL CRUSH YOU INTO . . ."

I couldn't hear the rest of the sentence because a huge wave hit me and knocked me into the sea.

SPLAAASH!

While I floundered in the water like a salmon going upstream, the waves pushed away our ONLY OAR!

"Since you're in the water, push the raft, smarty-mouseking!" Twisted Whisker yelled at me. "After all, it's your fault that we LOST the oar!"

I tried my best, clutching the raft and swimming with as much strength as I could muster.

"Go, Geronimo, go!" Trap shouted encouragingly. "You can do it, Cousin!"

But dry land seemed much too far away, and I was so exhausted! WHY, WHY, WHY wasn't I more athletic like Thora?

"Stop making all of that foam with your feet, smarty-pants!" Twisted Whisker shouted. "You don't want to attract a bunch of sharks, do you?"

"Sh-sh-sharks?" I stuttered fearfully.

Twisted Whisker snickered under his whiskers. Then he pointed to the horizon:

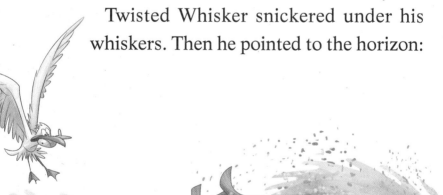

a **GRAY FIN** emerged from the sea and headed toward us.

"**HEEEELP!**" I shrieked. "**I DON'T WANT TO BE SHARK FOOD!**"

Wow, they're fast!

Uh-oh!

Shaaaarks?!

THE SIEGE OF THE DRAGONS

With the sharks on my tail, I swam like a *TORPEDO* through the icy-cold water of the fjord. My fear had **TURBO-CHARGED** my paws!

When we finally landed on a beach a short way from the port of Fearfjord, I was DRENCHED, exhausted, and in **Pain**, but luckily I still had all my fur!

"Wow, Cuz!" Trap remarked, chuckling. "Nothing can stop a mouseking, huh?"

"Yes, but . . . *pant, pant* . . . now I really need to catch . . . *pant, pant* . . . my breath!"

I spotted a soft bush nearby and threw myself down on the ground, leaning against the plant in utter exhaustion.

"**AAAAAAAAAAAAAAAAAAAAAAAAAAAAAH!**"

I yelped.

I had just sat down on a **pincushion**!

The little creature poked me with its long, sharp needles.

"**OW! OUCH! EEK!**" I squeaked. "**WHAT MOUSERIFIC PAIN!**"

THE PINCUSHION

The pincushion is the most docile animal on Miceking Island, but when it's scared, it puts up all of its sharp quills.

BE CAREFUL NOT TO MISTAKE IT FOR A BUSH!

I jumped back to my paws and heard
Twisted Whisker shriek, "**NOT THAT WAY,
COD SNOUT!**"

In my rush to get away from the pincushion,
I had landed right in a patch of stinging
nettles!

Squeak! The nettles made me ITCH like
crazy, more than a thousand fjord mosquito

I accidentally sat on a pincushion!

Ouchie!

bites! My fur felt like it was **ON FIRE**! How awful!

As soon as I got out of the stinging leaves, I joined the others. We moved slowly, making our way quietly toward the vileking village, sneaking through the sand and bushes and staying hidden from the view of any **dragons** flying overhead.

What an itch!

Then I wound up in some stinging nettles!

Unfortunately, a **terrifying** surprise awaited us in the village — it was entirely surrounded by enormouse, hungry, FIRE-SPITTING dragons!

Chartreuse and Crimson were among them. Suddenly, a 🐾🐾🐾 covered my mouth.

"Don't even think of making a squeak, mouseking," Twisted Whisker whispered in my ear. "You almost got us in BIG trouble back on Shipwreck Rock. So zip it unless you want to become a **mouse kabob**!"

Don't make a squeak!

I lay on the ground and tried to remain very still and quiet. But my whiskers continued to tremble with fear!

From our hiding

place, we could see that the **dragons** had roasted the roofs of the villages' houses, incinerated the tops of the trees, and reduced the vilekings' catapults to tiny bits of wood the size of seashells.

"Look!" Trap whispered as he **pointed** at the sky. Another group of dragons was **circling** over the village, observing everything.

"Wh-what do we do now?" I stuttered.

Thora held a finger to her lips. "Shhhh!" she replied. "Let's see if we can hear what those **slimy reptiles** are saying."

THORA'S DANGEROUS PLAN

While they were busy attacking the village of Fearfjord, the dragons continued to snarl at one another. In fact, those enormouse winged lizards had taken a break from burning the village to **fight** about how the vilekings should be prepared and eaten!

The red dragons rasped against the green ones. "I say that the

fatte**SSS**t mice should be eaten raw, **SSS**o they belong to us **DEVOURERSSS**!"

Chartreuse pawed the ground with his **CLAWS**, making everything around us tremble.

"And every Rinser knows that mice should fir**SSS**t be cleaned thoroughly, and then roasted to perfection!"

I'm right!

No, I am!

Introducing the Dragons!

At a glance, dragons may all seem alike, but never tell them that! In fact, different dragon families are very proud of their genealogy. If you confuse them, they may send a mouthful of fiery flames your way!

HERE'S HOW TO DISTINGUISH A RINSER FROM A DEVOURER!

RINSER

Once a Water Dragon captures a mouse, it prefers to rinse the mouse in a stagnant pond and then cook it before eating it.

DEVOURER

As soon as a Devourer captures a mouse, it eats it right away — raw, without even a side dish.

The Devourers hissed at the Rinsers. "Let us pa**SSS**, or you'll be in trouble!"

"No, you get out of our way!" the Rinsers replied.

"Don't you threaten u**SSS**!" Crimson yelled. "We're not moving unle**SSS** we **divide** the mice into equal part**SSS** fir**SSS**t!"

"Ugh, fine!" Chartreuse finally replied. "But if they e**SSS**cape, it'**SSS** all your fault!"

"All the mice are holed up in that hou**SSS**e down there," Crimson said, nodding his head. "They won't e**SSS**cape!"

"Did you hear that?" Twisted Whisker said happily. "The vilekings are hiding in the Hall of the Great Vileking Council. We must join them!"

"But how?" I asked, worried. "To enter the city we have to get past the dragons."

"And how would we hide from the dragons

that are **circling** overhead?" Trap added.

"**I have an idea!**" Thora exclaimed suddenly.

Thora's plan went like this:

1 To hide from the dragons, we would each hide inside one of the empty finnbrew barrels that were stacked outside the village.

2 Then we would slowly make our way to the Hall of the Great Vileking Council.

3 Finally, we would slip inside the building, where we would help the vilekings organize their **defense**.

It was a brilliant but very **DANGEROUS** plan!

"Cheesy catapults!" I exclaimed. "What if the dragons **discover** us? They'll capture us and roast us like **mouse kabobs**!"

But that dangerous plan was our only hope of saving the village of Fearfjord and the vilekings!

So, at **Twisted Whisker's** signal, we approached the barrels very quietly. Trap carved two holes in each barrel so that we could peer out and **SEE** where we were going.

Then, as quietly as mice, we each pulled a **BARREL** over our heads and silently inched our way toward the Hall of the Great Vileking Council.

Unfortunately for me, though, there was a seagull's nest on top of my barrel. And that **seagull** was not happy that her nest was **MOVING**! So the seagull began to make a fuss.

SQUAWK! SQUAWK! SQUAWK!

What's wrong with that seagull?

"Shoo, seagull!" I squeaked softly from inside my barrel. "They'll find us!"

But she continued to *flutter* around, squawking loudly.

That got Chartreuse's attention.

"What's wrong with that **SSS**eagull?" he growled.

Crimson also stopped and began to sniff the air.

Sniff! Sniff! Sniff!

"Hmmm . . ." he said. "I **SSS**mell fresh mou**SSS**e!"

Inside the barrel, I began to tremble.

Seconds later, all the **dragons** began

Well, what do we have here?

to **FOCUS** on the barrels!

"In my opinion, a mou**SSS**e i**SSS** playing hide-and-**SSS**eek in here!" Crimson said slyly as he **pawed** at my barrel.

At that point I had no choice but to **POP** out of the barrel and make a **break** for it.

"Good-bye, beautiful Thora!" I shrieked. **"Good-bye, friends! Good-bye world!"**

RUN, GERONIMO, RUN!

Once I popped out of my barrel, the dragons KNOCKED OVER the other barrels, revealing Thora, Trap, and Twisted Whisker.

CRASH! BANG! BOOM!

We found ourselves out in the open, helpless in front of that herd of scaly reptiles with OPEN, DROOLING jaws.

"What do we do now?" Trap yelled.

"**WE GET OUT OF HERE!**" Twisted Whisker shouted back.

So we scampered through the village as fast as we could, a pack of **ferocious** dragons

at our tails.

"They're e**SSS**caping!"

"Get tho**SSS**e mice!"

"Bite their tail**SSS**!"

We ran as fast as our little paws could carry us, but the dragons were much *FASTER*. They flew right above our heads, hissing tauntingly at us. "Come on, let'**SSS** eat them right here, right now!"

"Maybe we can still go back in the other direction," Twisted Whisker squeaked hopefully.

But unfortunately, **Crimson**, Chatreuse, and **Blue Villain** had come up behind us.

"There they are!" they shouted. "Let's **SSS**moke the chubby one and **SSS**auté the skinny ones!"

We were surrounded!

Trap hugged me tightly. "Geronimo, you've been the best cousin ever!" he gushed.

"You, too!" I blubbered.

A second later, the dragons closed in on us, their jaws DRIPPING with saliva.

But suddenly, I felt **two muscular paws** grab me and drag me away.

"This way, measly micekings!" a voice said.

In a second, we found ourselves safe inside a **cozy** mouse shop while outside the dragons continued to **fight**.

Safe by a whisker! But who had saved us?

There was only one other rodent in the shop with us, and he had LONG GRAY WHISKERS.

He was crawling around on the floor and seemed to be looking for something important.

"Wolfgang Ratson!" Twisted Whisker yelled. "Thank you for saving us!"

Huh?!

I was about to introduce myself, but Wolfgang motioned for us to be quiet. Then he pulled open a

TRAPDOOR hidden in the floor.

"Enough chatter!" he said gruffly. "Follow me!"

IT WAS A SECRET PASSAGE!

As we scurried down the hatch, the entire store began to tremble and **shake** as the dragons struck the building with their wings, tails, and claws.

Terrified, we followed Wolfgang down an **underground tunnel**!

THE GREAT
VILEKING COUNCIL

We continued **DOWN**, **DOWN**, **DOWN** the secret tunnel under the vileking village.

"This tunnel was excavated by Franz Ratson the First, the **great-great-great grandfather** of Ratnolf the Terrible . . ." Wolfgang explained.

"**WHERE** are we?" Trap asked.

"And where does this passage lead?" Thora added.

I was too scared and nervous to squeak! My paws trembled and my whiskers **wobbled** as I scurried after my friends.

When we arrived at the end of the tunnel, we went up a **long stone staircase**.

We're almost there!

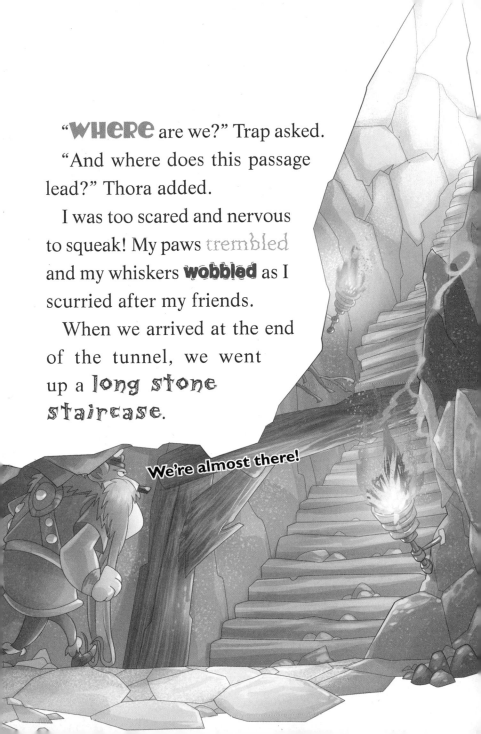

Finally, we came up in a very large room decorated with vileking shields and FLAGS.

It was the Hall of the Great Vileking Council! The citizens of Fearfjord were all HIDING there . . . really, all of them!

It was EXTREMELY CROWDED. It was so crowded that the knee of one Vileking was in my ear, the elbow of another bumped my snout, and the WHiSKeRS of who knows who were in my EYE!

Wolfgang scurried right up to Ratnolf the Terrible, who was sitting on a throne at the front of the room.

"Chief, I found Twisted Whisker," he

announced. "And these three puny micekings were with him!"

Ratnolf jumped up.

"Who told you to bring us other mice, Twisted Whisker?" he roared. "We're as tight as SALTED ANCHOVIES in a can here!"

"But, chief—" Twisted Whisker began, but Ratnolf cut him off.

"Silence!" Ratnolf bellowed. "Only I can speak, because I'm the MOST EVIL vileking around!"

RATNOLF THE TERRIBLE

He is the chief of the vilekings. If he gets angry, watch out! He prides himself on being incredibly evil. You'll recognize him by the patch on his eye. (He can see just fine, but he thinks it makes him look even scarier!)

Grrr! I'm the worst!

Everyone there repeated in unison:

"RATNOLF IS THE MOST EVIL VILEKING AROUND!"

"And what are you doing here, measly micekings?" Ratnolf asked, turning to us.

"We came to help you **DEFEAT** the dragons!" Thora responded testily.

"I, Ratnolf the Terrible, don't need anyone's help!" he roared back. "I am the strongest, the most courageous, and above all, **the most evil** vileking around!"

Again, the vilekings repeated in unison:

"RATNOLF IS THE MOST EVIL VILEKING AROUND!"

Then Thora saw Sven's mouseking helmet number forty-eight sitting on a **PEDESTAL**.

"That helmet belongs to my father, the courageous Sven the Shouter!" she cried. "You **STOLE** it, and I demand its return!"

"Silence!" Ratnolf roared. "That mouseking helmet belongs to me: **I** beat ten of the last twenty-one dragons in the famouse battle!"

But his wife, Mousegarde, intervened.

"This isn't the time to brag!" she yelled at her husband. "We are besieged by **dragons**! Accept their help!"

The chief of the vilekings sighed.

"Okay," he agreed reluctantly. Then he turned to me. "Let's hear your **PLAN**, mouseking!"

"P-plan?" I stuttered. "We have a p-plan?"

"Whaaat?!?" Ratnolf shouted **ANGRILY**. "Don't tell me you came here without a plan?!"

"Don't worry, I know what to do!" Trap

squeaked up, with a twinkle in his eye.

My whiskers began to tremble immediately. Whenever **Trap** has a plan, I'm usually the one whose *fur is on the line!*

My cousin showed us all a strange object made of branches and ropes. "We'll test my new invention: a pocket-sized CATAPULT that I call a slingshot!" Trap suggested.

When they saw Trap's slingshot, the vilekings began to snicker so loudly the

SLINGSHOT

This POCKET-SIZED CATAPULT is small, light, and easy to use (projectiles not included). It allows you to HIT THE TARGET with perfect precision (well, depending on your aim, ha!). Perfect for mice without muscles, as the projectiles are very light!

Hall of the Great Vileking Council began to **shake**.

"Shivering squids!" Ratnolf said, roaring with laughter. "Do you think you'll **SCARE** dragons with that gnat-sized gizmo?"

"Wait a minute!" I squeaked suddenly. "I just had a mouserific idea!"

What an idea!

SLINGSHOT ATTACK!

Ratnolf menacingly pointed his finger in front of my snout.

"And who would you be, puny rodent?" he growled.

"Geronimo is Mouseborg's resident scholar, and my father's trusted advisor," Thora squeaked quickly. "If he has something to say, it's best to listen to him!"

 Oh, beautiful Thora!

I couldn't believe my ears: The most courageous and fascinating rodent in Mouseborg was talking about **Me**! I smiled and stared at her.

"Well, hurry up, smarty-mouseking!"

Ratnolf yelled. "What are you waiting for? Tell us your idea!"

"Well, I noticed that there are a lot of nettle plants around here," I explained. "We could make balls out of the stinging leaves and launch them at the dragons with SLINGSHOTS! I landed in a nettle plant earlier myself, and great groaning glaciers, what a painful itch! The dragons would be miserable."

Trap gave me a pat on the back.

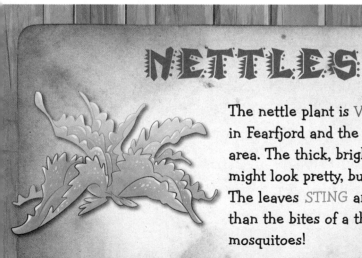

NETTLES

The nettle plant is VERY COMMON in Fearfjord and the surrounding area. The thick, bright-green bushes might look pretty, but watch out! The leaves STING and ITCH more than the bites of a thousand fjord mosquitoes!

"Great job, Cousin!" he said. "For once, you had a **good idea**!"

Mousegarde stepped forward.

"But how will we collect the nettle leaves?" she asked. "The dragons surround the village."

"We'll use the **SECRET PASSAGE**!" Wolfgang shouted.

Ratnolf raised his arm with a solemn gesture.

"I, Ratnolf the Terrible, order that we begin preparing for the **battle** against the dragons," he announced. "My courageous vilekings, let's chase away those awful reptiles!"

We all got to work: Trap **constructed** slingshots while the vilekings snuck away to gather the nettle leaves that are found around the village. The rest of us worked to transform the leaves into a **MOUNTAIN**

OF STINGING BALLS, ready for launch!

Soon it was time for the battle to begin. Thora, Trap, and I filed through the subterranean tunnel behind the vilekings, and we gathered in the center of the village.

Luckily, the **dragons** were still arguing and they didn't notice us.

Ratnolf had explained the battle strategy to us in the cave. "You micekings from Mouseborg will **ATTACK** the dragons with the slingshots," he explained. "Meanwhile, the ferocious vilekings will distract the dragons!"

Now I was a little worried about the plan.

"How is this going to work?" I asked nervously as we took our positions.

"That doesn't concern you, smartymouseking," Ratnolf sneered. "Just stay out of the way while we vilekings distract the **ENEMY**!"

Get down!

Take that!

Sorry!

Ouch!

Mousegarde had agreed to accompany us to the roofs of Fearfjord. She climbed fearlessly up a *rope ladder*, and Thora, Trap, and I scampered after her. As soon as we were in position . . .

ROOOOOOOAAAAARRR!

The sound of a dragon made my whiskers shake. Below us, the vilekings gathered in the center of town, **frozen** like immobile blocks of rock.

Then, while Mousegarde, Thora, Trap, and I took aim from the rooftops, the vilekings began to do an incredible dance!

They shook their paws, pulled their whiskers, and YELLED AT THE TOPS OF THEIR LUNGS:

"UUUUURGHH-AAARGH! OOOGAH-BOO!

WATCH YOUR TAILS OR WE'LL CRUSH YOU!

WE ARE VILEKINGS, HEAR US ROAR,

WATCH AS WE WAVE OUR PAWS!

WE'RE VILE, MEAN, AND FEROCIOUS, TOO,

UUUUURGHH-AAARGH! OOOGAH-BOO!"

The dragons stared with JAWS OPEN: They couldn't believe their ears! It really was a bizarre spectacle!

Only Blue Villain raised her head to the rooftops and saw us, but by that point it was too late. On Trap's signal, we bombarded the dragons with a storm of nettle balls!

The dragons scratched themselves furiously: under their eyes, behind their ears, on their tails . . . everywhere!

"Retreat!" Chartreuse finally hissed. "I'm **sss**o itchy! I need a thermal **sss**ulfur bath immediately!"

Behind him, the dragons fluttered away one after the other, shrieking in pain.

As they escaped, Ratnolf yelled after them, "And don't come back, you rotten reptiles!"

The siege of the dragons had failed!

I'm Too Fond of My Fur!

In the end, the battle of Fearfjord was a huge success for the micekings and the vilekings. However, we micekings still had another task: retrieving the *stolen* helmet!

Ratnolf was waiting for us in the center of town on a **PEDESTAL** being held up by two burly vilekings.

We won!

"Now that the village of Fearfjord is safe, we ask you to return my father's mouseking helmet," Thora announced for all to hear.

Ratnolf ignored her. "Mice of Fearfjord, we have won!" he declared. "To celebrate, you are all invited to a **delicious vileking banquet!**"

"Wait a minute, Ratnolf!" Mousegarde intervened. "You haven't answered Thora yet. This invitation to the banquet is just **an excuse** to postpone returning Sven the Shouter's helmet!"

"But I —"

"Be quiet!" Mousegarde interrupted her husband. "**NO EXCUSES!** A village chief that is worthy of respect must be strong, courageous, and above all, **fair!**"

So in the end, Ratnolf gave **MOUSEKING HELMET NUMBER FORTY-EIGHT** back to Thora.

"Even if we didn't ask for your help, and we would have **squashed** those dragons on our own . . . **thanks**!" he grumbled. "And this isn't the end of my **feud** with Sven the Shouter, that's for sure!"

Then he gave me a package tied with a

Here's the helmet . . .

THICK cord. "I have an important task for you, smarty-mouseking," he said mysteriously.

"Please give this **gift** to Sven the Shouter from me. He'll be very **SURPRISED**."

I felt proud to have such an important role to play: **What a great mouseking honor!**

"Now, while we wait for the banquet to be ready, let's have a VILEKING CHALLENGE!" Ratnolf shouted. "Who's up for the pincushion jump, followed by a swimming race with some sharks, and a diving contest off the Cliffs of Fear? Let's show the little mice of Mouseborg how strong the **VILEKINGS** really are!"

I immediately thought of the shipwreck on the reef, the **sharks**, my dive into the nettle bushes, and the fire-breathing dragons. I'd already had enough Vileking Challenges to last a lifetime!

HERE ARE THE MOST FAMOUSE VILEKING CHALLENGES . . .

DIVING OFF THE CLIFFS OF FEAR

PINCUSHION JUMP

SWIMMING RACE WITH SHARKS

"**Noooooo, THANKS!**" I yelled as I scampered to the back of the crowd. "I'm too fond of my fur for a Vileking Challenge!"

Great groaning glaciers! If that's what it took to earn a mouseking helmet, I would never get one . . . I'm too much of a scaredy-mouse!

FORGET ABOUT THE HELMET!

With the help of the vilekings, we repaired the *Bated Breath*, said good-bye, and set sail for home. When we docked in the port of Mouseborg, the entire village was there waiting for us.

I'm so proud of you!

Sven the Shouter himself came to meet us on the pier.

"So?" he asked expectantly. "Did you bring back my **MOUSEKING HELMET**?"

"Yes, of course!" Thora replied confidently. And we also saved the village of Fearfjord from the dragons!"

"Good job!" Sven congratulated his daughter. "You've demonstrated to Ratnolf how to act like a **true mouseking**! I've decided to award you with a mouseking helmet!"

"**YAY!**" the crowd cheered. "A mouseking

helmet for Thora! **Hooray!**"

"We'll celebrate with a mouseking-erific banquet," Sven continued. "After that, we'll finally see the real THREE MOUSEKINGETEERS in action!"

"There's just one more thing," Thora insisted. "Shouldn't GERONIMO get a small mouseking helmet, too? It was his idea to use the nettle leaves against the dragons."

Sven thought about it.

"Well, maybe . . ." he said hesitantly.

At that moment, I remembered the vileking PACKAGE I was supposed to deliver.

"Sven, I have a gift for you from Ratnolf!" I said.

Sven took the package, opened it, and . . .

PUFF!

A cloud of chopped nettle leaves hit him right in the face!

Oh no! All the mice around him began to scratch themselves desperately!

"Forget about the helmet, smarty-mouseking!" Sven shouted furiously.

"B-but I d-didn't have anything to do with it!" I argued. WHY, WHY, WHY does everything always happen to me?

I sighed. At least I had fought bravely next to the courageous Thora! And sooner or later, I would earn my own mouseking helmet — I just knew it!

BUT THAT'S A STORY FOR ANOTHER DAY — MOUSEKING'S HONOR!

Get away!
What a terrible prank!
What is it?
It's stinging nettle leaves!
Oh no!
Huh?!

Don't miss any adventures of the Micekings!

#1 Attack of the Dragons

#2 The Famouse Fjord Race

#3 Pull the Dragon's Tooth!

#4 Stay Strong, Geronimo!

#5 The Mysterious Message

#6 The Helmet Holdup

Up Next:

#7 The Dragon Crown

Be sure to read all my fabumouse adventures!

#1 Lost Treasure of the Emerald Eye

#2 The Curse of the Cheese Pyramid

#3 Cat and Mouse in a Haunted House

#4 I'm Too Fond of My Fur!

#5 Four Mice Deep in the Jungle

#6 Paws Off, Cheddarface!

#7 Red Pizzas for a Blue Count

#8 Attack of the Bandit Cats

#9 A Fabumouse Vacation for Geronimo

#10 All Because of a Cup of Coffee

#11 It's Halloween, You 'Fraidy Mouse!

#12 Merry Christmas, Geronimo!

#13 The Phantom of the Subway

#14 The Temple of the Ruby of Fire

#15 The Mona Mousa Code

#16 A Cheese-Colored Camper

#17 Watch Your Whiskers, Stilton!

#18 Shipwreck on the Pirate Islands

#19 My Name Is Stilton, Geronimo Stilton

#20 Surf's Up, Geronimo!

#21 The Wild, Wild West

#22 The Secret of Cacklefur Castle

A Christmas Tale

#23 Valentine's Day
Disaster

#24 Field Trip to
Niagara Falls

#25 The Search for
Sunken Treasure

#26 The Mummy
with No Name

#27 The Christmas
Toy Factory

#28 Wedding
Crasher

#29 Down and Out
Down Under

#30 The Mouse Island
Marathon

#31 The Mysterious
Cheese Thief

Christmas Catastrophe

#32 Valley of the
Giant Skeletons

#33 Geronimo and the
Gold Medal Mystery

#34 Geronimo Stilton,
Secret Agent

#35 A Very Merry
Christmas

#36 Geronimo's
Valentine

#37 The Race Across
America

#38 A Fabumouse
School Adventure

#39 Singing Sensation

#40 The Karate Mouse

#41 Mighty Mount
Kilimanjaro

#42 The Peculiar
Pumpkin Thief

#43 I'm Not a
Supermouse!

#44 The Giant
Diamond Robbery

#45 Save the White
Whale!

#46 The Haunted
Castle

#47 Run for the Hills, Geronimo!

#48 The Mystery in Venice

#49 The Way of the Samurai

#50 This Hotel Is Haunted!

#51 The Enormouse Pearl Heist

#52 Mouse in Space!

#53 Rumble in the Jungle

#54 Get into Gear, Stilton!

#55 The Golden Statue Plot

#56 Flight of the Red Bandit

#57 The Stinky Cheese Vacation

#58 The Super Chef Contest

#59 Welcome to Moldy Manor

#60 The Treasure of Easter Island

#61 Mouse House Hunter

#62 Mouse Overboard!

#63 The Cheese Experiment

#64 Magical Mission

#65 Bollywood Burglary

#66 Operation: Secret Recipe

#67 The Chocolate Chase

#68 Cyber-Thief Showdown

Up Next:

#69 Hug A Tree, Geronimo

THE KINGDOM OF FANTASY

THE QUEST FOR PARADISE:
THE RETURN TO THE KINGDOM OF FANTASY

Don't miss any of my special edition adventures!

THE AMAZING VOYAGE:
THE THIRD ADVENTURE IN THE KINGDOM OF FANTASY

THE DRAGON PROPHECY:
THE FOURTH ADVENTURE IN THE KINGDOM OF FANTASY

THE VOLCANO OF FIRE:
THE FIFTH ADVENTURE IN THE KINGDOM OF FANTASY

THE SEARCH FOR TREASURE:
THE SIXTH ADVENTURE IN THE KINGDOM OF FANTASY

THE ENCHANTED CHARMS:
THE SEVENTH ADVENTURE IN THE KINGDOM OF FANTASY

THE PHOENIX OF DESTINY:
AN EPIC KINGDOM OF FANTASY ADVENTURE

THE HOUR OF MAGIC:
THE EIGHTH ADVENTURE IN THE KINGDOM OF FANTASY

THE WIZARD'S WAND:
THE NINTH ADVENTURE IN THE KINGDOM OF FANTASY

THE SHIP OF SECRETS:
THE TENTH ADVENTURE IN THE KINGDOM OF FANTASY

THE DRAGON OF FORTUNE:
AN EPIC KINGDOM OF FANTASY ADVENTURE

THE JOURNEY THROUGH TIME

BACK IN TIME:
THE SECOND JOURNEY THROUGH TIME

THE RACE AGAINST TIME:
THE THIRD JOURNEY THROUGH TIME

LOST IN TIME:
THE FOURTH JOURNEY THROUGH TIME

Up Next!

NO TIME TO LOSE:
THE FIFTH JOURNEY THROUGH TIME

Meet
GERONIMO STILTONOOT

He is a cavemouse — Geronimo Stilton's ancient ancestor! He runs the stone newspaper in the prehistoric village of Old Mouse City. From dealing with dinosaurs to dodging meteorites, his life in the Stone Age is full of adventure!

#1 The Stone of Fire

#2 Watch Your Tail!

#3 Help, I'm in Hot Lava!

#4 The Fast and the Frozen

#5 The Great Mouse Race

#6 Don't Wake the Dinosaur!

#7 I'm a Scaredy-Mouse!

#8 Surfing for Secrets

#9 Get the Scoop, Geronimo!

#10 My Autosaurus Will Win!

#11 Sea Monster Surprise

#12 Paws Off the Pearl!

#13 The Smelly Search

#14 Shoo, Caveflies!

#15 A Mammoth Mystery

MEET
GERONIMO STILTONIX

He is a spacemouse — the Geronimo Stilton of a parallel universe! He is captain of the spaceship *MouseStar 1*. While flying through the cosmos, he visits distant planets and meets crazy aliens. His adventures are out of this world!

#1 Alien Escape

#2 You're Mine, Captain!

#3 Ice Planet Adventure

#4 The Galactic Goal

#5 Rescue Rebellion

#6 The Underwater Planet

#7 Beware! Space Junk!

#8 Away in a Star Sled

#9 Slurp Monster Showdown

#10 Pirate Spacecat Attack

#11 We'll Bite Your Tail, Geronimo!

#12 The Invisible Planet

Dear mouse friends,
thanks for reading,

and good-bye until
the next book!